S0-EMB-215

BRANCH SHIPMENTS:

ARC_____
BLK_____
FER_____
FOR_____
GAR_____
HOA_____
KTR_____
MCK_____
RDL_____
TRD_____
BKM_____

Learning How to Feel Good About Yourself

Susan Kent

The Rosen Publishing Group's
PowerKids Press™
New York

For Karl Bissinger, who makes everyone feel good.

Published in 2001 by The Rosen Publishing Group, Inc.
29 East 21st Street, New York, NY 10010

First Edition

Book Design: Maria E. Melendez

Photo Credits: Cover and title page, pp. 4, 7, 8, 11, 12, 15, 16, 19, 20 by Myles Pinkney

Kent, Susan, 1942–
    Learning how to feel good about yourself / by Susan Kent.
        p. cm.— (The violence prevention library)
    Includes index.
    Summary: Describes how children can boost their self-esteem by doing things they enjoy and are good at and by seeking the advice and comfort of others.
    ISBN 0-8239-5615-6
    1. Self-esteem in children—Juvenile literature. [1. Self-esteem.] I. Title. II. Series.
    BF723.S3.K46 2000
    158.1'083'4—dc21   99-056848

Manufactured in the United States of America

Contents

When You Feel Bad

We would all like to feel good all the time, but many things can happen that make us feel bad. If you get teased, do poorly in school, or do not make the soccer team, you might feel bad about yourself. You might think you cannot do anything right. At times like these, other people can help you feel better. Your family can offer comfort and advice. Your friends can cheer you up. Your teachers can give you extra help in school. Do not forget, though, that there are lots of things you can do to feel good about yourself.

◀ *This boy feels bad because he failed his test.*

Pete

Pete feels sad when kids tease him for striking out four times in one baseball game. When he gets home, he practices his guitar. After a while, playing the guitar helps him feel better. He also talks to his parents. They tell him they love him. They say it is okay that he is not the greatest baseball player. They remind him that he is an excellent musician. Pete thinks about some of the other things he is good at, like math. He is also a good friend. He and his friend Mario have fun playing the guitar together. Pete goes to bed feeling much better about himself.

It is important to do activities that make you feel good about yourself. ▶

Noticing Your Talents

One of the first things you can do to feel good about yourself is to pay attention to what you do well. Some talents are easy to **recognize**, like drawing or singing. There are other things, though, that you might be good at and do not realize. You might be a hard worker. You might solve problems well or make the right choices for yourself. You might be responsible and do all your chores. You might be a kind person and a caring friend. Be sure to remind yourself of all these special skills. When you do, you will feel good about yourself.

We all have special talents that make us
◄ *feel good about ourselves.*

Being Proud of Yourself

You may feel proud when you get a good grade on a test or do well in a sports game. There are many other things, though, to feel proud about. When you try hard at whatever you do, you have reason to feel proud. You can also feel proud when you try new things. This is not always easy. You might be afraid of failing. You might worry that people will make fun of you. It is natural to feel nervous when you try something new. The only way you can learn new skills, though, is to give it your best shot. You can feel good knowing you are trying to do your best.

You should be proud of yourself when you try something new, like swimming. ▶

Complimenting Yourself

Compliment yourself when you do something well. You do not have to wait for other people to say it for you. Tell yourself "Good job!" when you do a good job. **Congratulate** yourself when you do well on a spelling test or sing a good solo in chorus. When you make a new friend, write a funny story, or read a great book, tell yourself how kind, clever, or smart you are. Do not worry that this will make you **conceited**. You are just recognizing your **accomplishments**. Letting yourself know you have done well helps you feel good about yourself.

When you win an award, tell yourself you did a good job.

Treat Yourself Well

Another way to feel good about yourself is to treat yourself well. Find time to relax. Take time out during the day to do what you like to do. You might like to read or write. Maybe you like to think or daydream. Some people love to relax by listening to music or taking a walk in a pretty park. If your friends want to go to the mall, but you feel like drawing, stay home and make sketches of your cat sleeping in the sun. Doing what matters to you helps you become the person you want to be. Being the person you want to be helps you feel good about yourself.

Take time out for yourself and do things that make you happy. ▶

Doing What Is Right for You

It is important to do what feels right for you, even when that makes you different. Students sometimes feel **pressure** to be like the other kids. No two people are alike, though. Some like sports. Others would rather read lots of books. Some like to hang out in a big crowd. Others prefer to spend time in a small group. Everyone has his or her own hopes and dreams. You might hope to become a dancer or a firefighter. Maybe your friend wants to be a teacher or a basketball player. When you do what is right for you, you can feel good about yourself.

◀ *Following your dreams will help you feel good about yourself.*

When You Make Mistakes

We all make mistakes, sometimes even when we know better. You might get angry and throw something. You might tease a classmate who stutters. Doing what you know is wrong usually makes you feel bad about yourself. A good way to get back your **self-respect** is to say you are sorry. Tell people you feel bad when you hurt their feelings. Try to make up for your mistakes by doing something nice for the person you upset. When you say you are sorry, you make the person you hurt feel better. You also feel good about yourself again.

Saying you are sorry for a mistake helps everyone feel better. ▶

Helping Other People

A great way to feel good about yourself is to help others. If someone drops her lunch tray, do not laugh. Instead help her clean it up. When new students come to your school, make them feel welcome. If you see classmates being left out of activities, invite them to join in the fun. It is also important to stand up for what you think is right. If you notice a group of kids picking on someone, tell them to stop being mean. Always try to **defend** someone who is being hurt or picked on. Not only will you feel good about yourself, others will **admire** you, too.

◀ *Helping other people will help you feel good, too.*

Mark and Felicia

Mark and Felicia do not feel safe at school because gangs there pick on the kids who are different from them. With the help of their **guidance counselor**, they form a Let's Be Safe club. Lots of their classmates join. They have meetings, make posters, and get everyone to talk about the problem. Soon their school is a safer place. Mark and Felicia feel proud of what they started. You will always feel good about yourself when you stand up for what you believe is right.

Glossary

accomplishments (ak-KOM-plish-ments) Things a person finishes successfully.

admire (ad-MYR) To respect or like very much.

compliment (KOHM-pluh-ment) To tell someone that he or she is doing a good job.

conceited (kon-SEET-ed) Thinking that you are better than other people.

congratulate (kun-GRA-joo-layt) To tell someone you are proud of something he or she did.

defend (dih-FEND) To protect from attack or harm.

guidance counselor (GY-dins KOWN-suh-ler) Someone who helps students solve personal problems or problems with other people.

pressure (PREH-shur) The weight of feeling worried about something you have to do.

recognize (REH-kig-nyz) To know someone or something.

self-respect (SELF-ree-SPEKT) Thinking highly of yourself.

Index